Nursery
Rhymes.

Cock Robin
and
Jenny Wren.

Young Canada's Nursery Rhymes.

Illustrated
by
Constance Haslewood.

KPk
Key Porter Kids

Originally published by Frederick Warne & Co., London and New York, 1897

ISBN 1-55263-116-8
CIP Data available upon request

Key Porter Books Limited
70 The Esplanade
Toronto, Ontario
Canada M5E 1R2

Printed and bound in Italy

A was an Apple pie;

B bit it;
C cut it;
D dealt it;
E eat it;
F fought for it;
G got it;
H had it;
J joined it;
K kept it;
L longed for it;
M mourned for it;
N nodded at it;
O opened it;
P peeped in it;
Q quartered it;
R ran for it;
S stole it;
T took it;
V viewed it;
W wanted it;
X, Y, Z, and &, all wish'd for a piece in hand.

There was a crooked man, and he went a crooked
mile,
He found a crooked sixpence against a crooked stile:
He bought a crooked cat, which caught a crooked
mouse,
And they all lived together in a little crooked house.

Curly locks, curly locks, wilt thou be mine?
Thou shalt not wash dishes, nor yet feed the swine;
But sit on a cushion, and sew a fine seam,
And feed upon strawberries, sugar, and cream.

My little old man and I fell out,
I'll tell you what it was all about;
I had money and he had none,
And that's the way the noise begun.

Bow-wow-wow, whose dog art thou?
Little Tom Tucker's dog, bow-wow-wow.

Multiplication is vexation,
Division is as bad;
The Rule of Three doth puzzle me,
And Practice drives me mad.

See a pin and pick it up,
All the day you'll have good luck;
See a pin and let it lay,
Bad luck you'll have all the day.

Jack Sprat could eat no fat,
His wife could eat no lean;
And so betwixt them both, you see,
They made the platter clean.

(A STAR)

Higher than a house, higher than a tree;
Oh! whatever can that be?

Little Miss Muffett
She sat on a tuffett,
Eating of curds
and whey;

There came a great
spider
Who sat down
beside her,
And frightened
Miss Muffett
away.

Little Bo-peep
has lost her sheep,
And cannot tell
where to find them;

Leave them alone,
and they'll come home,
And bring their
tails
behind them.

1. This pig went to market;
2. This pig stayed at home;
3. This pig had a bit of meat;
4. And this pig had none;
5. This pig said, Wee, wee, wee!
6. I can't find my way home.

Little Polly Flinders
Sate among the cinders
Warming her pretty little toes!
Her mother came and caught her,
And whipped her little daughter,
For spoiling her nice new clothes.

Dance little baby, dance up high,
Never mind baby, mother is nigh;
Crow and caper, caper and crow,
There little baby, there ... you go;
Up to the ceiling, down to the ground
Backwards and forwards, round and round.
Dance little baby mother will sing,
With the merry coral, ding, ding, ding.

Here sits the Lord Mayor .... *forehead.*
Here sits his two men .... *eyes.*
Here sits the cock .... *right cheek.*
Here sits the hen .... *left cheek.*
Here sit the little chickens ...... *tip of nose.*
Here they run in .... *mouth.*
Chin-chopper, chin-chopper, chin-
chopper, chin! .... *chuck the chin.*

To market, To market,
to buy a fat pig,
Home again, home again,
jiggety jig.
To market, To market,
to buy a fat hog,
Home again, home again,
jiggety jog.

Jack and Jill
went up the hill,
To fetch a pail of water;
Jack fell down,
and broke his crown,
And Jill came
tumbling
after.

Swan, swan, over the sea;

Swim, swan, swim.

Swan, swan, back again;

Well swam, swan.

Humpty-Dumpty sat on a wall,
Humpty-Dumpty had a great fall;
All the king's horses, and all the king's men,
Cannot put Humpty-Dumpty together again.

I had a little hobby horse,
And it was dapple grey;
Its head was made of pea-straw,
Its tail was made of hay.
I sold it to an old woman
For a copper groat;
And I'll not sing my song again
Without a new coat

Handy Spandy, Jack-a-dandy,
Loves plum-cake and sugar-candy;
He bought some at a grocer's shop,
And out he came, hop-hop-hop.

Jack be nimble, Jack be quick;
And Jack jump over the candlestick.

Little Tom Tucker sings for his supper;
What shall he eat? White bread an butter.
How shall he cut it without e'er a knife?
How will he marry without e'er a wife?

Three straws on a staff
Would make a baby cry and laugh.

Ride a cock horse to Banbury Cross,
To see an old lady ride on a white horse,
Rings on her fingers and bells on her toes.
So she makes music wherever she goes.

How many days has my baby to play?
Saturday, Sunday, Monday,
Tuesday, Wednesday, Thursday, Friday,
Saturday, Sunday, Monday.

Dickery,

Dickery,

Dock!

The mouse ran up the clock;

The clock struck

One!

And down the mouse ran,

Dickery,

Dickery,

Dock!

Some little mice
sat in a barn to spin;
Pussy came by,
and popped her head in;
"Shall I come in,
and cut your threads off?"
"Oh, no, kind sir,
you will snap our heads off!"

Needles and pins, needles and pins,
When a man marries his trouble begins.

Deedle, deedle, dumpling, my son John,
He went to bed with his stockings on;
One shoe off, and one shoe on,
Deedle, deedle, dumpling, my son John,

All of a row, bend the bow;
Shot at a pigeon and killed a crow.

You shall have a fish, in a little dish,
You shall have a fish, when the boat comes in.

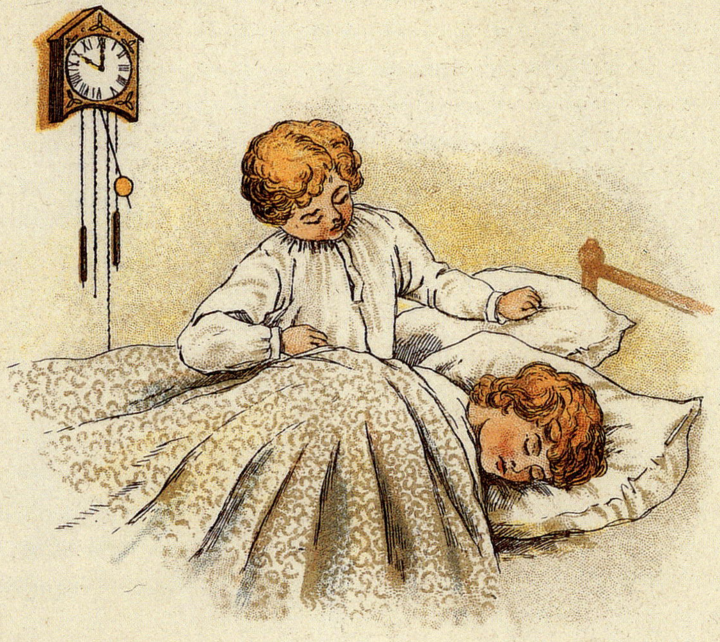

Robin and Richard were two pretty men,
They laid in bed till the clock struck ten;
Then up starts Robin, and looks in the sky,
"Oh, brother Richard, the sun's very high!
The bull's in the barn threshing the corn;
The cock's on the hayrick blowing his horn."

The Queen of Hearts, she made some tarts,
All on a summer's day;
The knave of Hearts, he stole the tarts,
And took them clean away.

Sing a song of sixpence, a bag full of Rye,
Four-and-twenty Blackbirds baked in a Pie;
When the Pie was opened, the Birds began to sing,
Was not that a dainty dish to set before a King?

Young lambs to sell, young lambs to sell;
If I had as much money as I could tell,
I never would cry, young lambs to sell.
Young lambs to sell, young lambs to sell,
I never would cry, young lambs to sell.

Ding, dong, bell; Pussy's in the well.
Who put her in? Little Tommy Green.
Who pulled her out? Little Tommy Trout.
What a naughty boy was that,
To drown poor Pussy Cat.

Polly, put the kettle on,
Polly, put the kettle on,
Polly, put the kettle on,
And let's drink tea.
Sukey, take it off again,
Sukey, take it off again,
Sukey, take it off again,
They're all gone away.

Pussy-cat, Pussy-cat
where have you been?
I've been to London
to look at the Queen

Pussy-cat, Pussy-cat,
what did you there?
I frightened
a little mouse
under
the chair.

Blow, wind blow—
And go, mill, go—
That the miller
May grind his corn;

That the baker may
take it,
And into rolls make it,
And bring us some
hot in the morn.

Mary had a pretty bird,
Feathers bright and yellow,
Slender legs — upon my word
He was a pretty fellow.

The sweetest notes
he always sung,
Which much delighted
Mary;
And near the cage
she'd often sit
To hear her own
canary

Tom he was a piper's son,
He learned to play when he was young,
But all the tunes that he could play,
Was "Over the hills and far away."
Tom with his pipe did play with such skill,
That those who heard him could never keep still;
Whenever they heard him they began to dance,
Even pigs on their hind legs would
after him prance.

I saw a ship a-sailing,
A-sailing on the sea
And, oh! it was all laden
With pretty things for thee.
There were comfits in the cabin
And apples in the hold,

The sails were made
of silk,
The masts were made
of gold.

What's the news of the day, good neighbour, I pray?
They say the balloon is gone up to the moon.

There were two birds sat on a stone,
Fa, la, la, la, lal, de;
One flew away, and then there was one,
Fa, la, la, la, lal, de;
The other flew after, and then there was none,
Fa, la, la, la, lal, de;
And so the poor stone was left all alone,
Fa, la, la, la, lal, de!

A sunshiny shower
Won't last half an hour.

Leg over leg, as the dog went to Dover;
When he came to a style, jump he went over.

Peter Piper picked a peck of pickled pepper;
A peck of pickled pepper Peter Piper picked;
If Peter Piper picked a peck of pickled pepper,
Where's the peck of pickled pepper Peter Piper picked?

Hush a bye,
Baby
On the tree top,

When the wind blows
the cradle will rock:
When the bough bends
the cradle will fall.
Down will come
Baby
cradle
and all.

Matthew
Mark,
Luke,
And John.
Guard the bed that I lie on
Four corners to my bed,
Four angels round my head,
One to watch, and one to pray,
And two to bear my soul
away.

Three wise men of Gotham
Went to sea in a bowl:
And if the bowl had been stronger,
My song would have been longer.

Doctor Foster went to Gloster,
In a shower of rain;
He stepped in a puddle, up to the middle,
And never went there again.

There was an old woman tossed up in a basket,
Ninety times as high as the moon;
And where she was going, I couldn't but ask it,
For in her hand she carried a broom.

Old woman, old woman, old woman, quoth I,
O whither, O whither, O whither, so high?
To sweep the cobwebs off the sky!
Shall I go with you? Aye, by and by.

Once I saw a little bird
Come hop, hop, hop;
So I cried "Little bird,
Will you stop, stop, stop?"
And was going to the window
To say "How do you do?"
But he shook his little tail,
And far away he flew.

Is John Smith within? Yes, that he is.
Can he set a shoe? Ay, marry, two;
Here a nail, there a nail, tick, tack, too.

See, see. What shall I see?
A horse's head where his tail should be.

I like little Pussy, her coat is so warm,
And if I don't hurt her she'll do me no harm;
So I'll not pull her tail, nor drive her away,
But Pussy and I very gently will play.

Go to bed first, a golden purse
Go to bed second, a golden pheasant;
Go to bed third, a golden bird.

Goosey, Goosey, gander, whither shall I wander?
Upstairs, and downstairs, and in my lady's chamber.
There I met an old man, who would not say his
prayers,
I took him by the left leg, and threw him down stairs.

The cock doth crow to let you know,
If you be wise, 't is time to rise.

Eat, birds, eat, and make no waste,
I lie here and make no haste;
If my master chance to come,
You must fly, and I must run.

Where are you going to, my pretty maid?
I am going a milking, sir, she said.
May I go with you, my pretty maid?
You're kindly welcome, sir, she said.

Shoe the wild horse, and shoe the grey mare,
If the horse wont be shod, let him go bare.

Bye, baby bunting,
Father's gone a hunting,
Mother's gone a milking,
Sister's gone a silking,
Brother's gone to buy a skin
To wrap the baby bunting in.

Daffy-down-Dilly has come up to town,
In a yellow petticoat and a green gown.

Ba-a, ba-a, black sheep,
have you any wool?
Yes, sir, yes, sir,
three bags full:
One for my master,
one for my dame,
And one for the little boy
that lives in our lane.

As I was going up Pippen Hill,
Pippen Hill was dirty,
There I met a pretty miss,
And she dropped me a curtsey.

Little miss, pretty miss,
Blessings shine upon you!
If I had half a crown a day,
I'd spend it all upon you.

Ride a cock-horse to Banbury Cross,
To see what Tommy can buy;
A penny white loaf, a penny white cake,
And a twopenny apple pie.

See, saw, Margery Daw,
Jenny shall have a new master;
She shall have but a penny a day,
Because she can't work any faster.

When I was a bachelor, I lived by myself,
And all the meat I got, I put upon the shelf;
The rats and the mice did lead me such a life,
That I went to London to get myself a wife,
The streets were so broad and the lanes were so narrow,
I could not get my wife home without a wheelbarrow;
The wheelbarrow broke, my wife got a fall,
Down tumbled wheelbarrow, little wife and all.

I had a little pony,
  His name was Dapple-gray,
I lent him to a lady,
  To ride a mile away.
She whipped him, she slashed him,
  She rode him through the mire;
I would not lend my pony now
  For all the lady's hire

Come, let's to bed,
Says Sleepy Head,
Tarry a while,
Says Slow;
Put on the pan,
Says Greedy Nan,
Let's sup before we go.

Simple Simon met a pieman,
Going to the fair;
Says Simple Simon to the pieman,
"Let me taste your ware."
Says the pieman to Simple Simon,
"Show me first your penny."
Says Simple Simon
to the pieman,
"Indeed, I have not any."

Cock-a-doodle-doo!
My dame has lost her shoe;
My master's lost his fiddling stick,
And don't know what to do.

Cock-a-doodle-doo!
What is my dame to do?
Till master finds his fiddling stick,
She'll dance without her shoe.

Little Robin Redbreast sat upon a tree,
Up went Pussy-cat, and down went he;
Down came Pussy-cat, and away Robin ran;
Says little Robin Redbreast, "Catch me if you
can."
Little Robin Redbreast flew upon a wall,
Pussy-cat jumped after him, and almost got a
fall;
Little Robin chirp'd and sang, and what did
Pussy say?
Pussy-cat said "Mew," and Robin flew away.

A little cock-sparrow sat on a tree,
Looking as happy as happy could be,
Till a boy came by, with his bow and arrow,
Says he, I will shoot the little cock-sparrow.

His body will make me a nice little stew,
And his giblets will make me a little pie, too.
Says the little cock-sparrow, I'll be shot if I stay,
So he clapped his wings and then flew away.

Cuckoo, cherry tree,
Catch a bird, and give it me.
Let the tree be high or low,
Let it hail, rain, or snow.

There was a little man, and he had a little gun,
And his bullets were made of lead, lead, lead;
He shot Johnny Sprig through the middle of his wig,
And knocked it right off his head, head, head.

Pat a cake, pat a cake, baker's man,
Bake me a cake as fast as you can;
Pat it and prick it and mark it with T,
And put in the oven for Tommy and me.

Taffy was a Welshman, Taffy was a thief;
Taffy came to my house and stole a piece of beef;
I went to Taffy's house, Taffy was not at home;
Taffy came to my house and stole a marrow bone.

In the merry month of May
When green leaves begin to spring,
Little lambs do skip like fairies,
Birds do couple, build, and sing.

(An Egg.)

In marble walls as white as milk,
Lined with a skin as soft as silk;
Within a fountain crystal clear,
A golden apple doth appear,
No doors there are to this stronghold,
Yet things break in and steal the gold.

Little Cock Robin peeped out of his nest,
To see the cold winter come in,
Tit for tat, what matter for that,
He'll hide his head under his wing!

Thirty days hath September,
April, June, and November;
February has twenty-eight alone;
All the rest have thirty-one,
Excepting leap-year—that's the time
When February's days are twenty-nine.

The man in the wilderness asked me,
How many strawberries grew in the sea;
I answered him, as I thought good,
As many as red herrings grew in the wood.

Molly, my sister, and I fell out,
And what do you think it was about?
She loved coffee, and I loved tea,
And that was the reason we could not agree.

My maid Mary, she minds her dairy,
While I go hoeing and mowing each morn;
Merrily run the reel and the little spinning wheel,
Whilst I am singing and mowing my corn.

A little boy went into a barn,
And lay down on some hay;
An owl came out and flew about,
And the little boy ran away.

Mary, Mary,

quite contrary,

How does your garden grow?

Silver bells,

and cockle shells

and pretty maids

all in a row.

Little girl, little girl,
where have you been?
Gathering roses to give to the Queen.
Little girl, little girl,
what gave she you?
She gave me a diamond
as big as my shoe.

Diddledy,
Diddledy,
Dumpty:
The cat ran up the plum tree.
I'll wager a crown
I'll fetch you down;
Sing, diddledy,
Diddledy,
Dumpty.

I'll sing you a song
Though not very long
Yet I think it
As pretty as any

Put your hand
in your purse
You'll never be worse
And give the poor singer
A penny.

Rain, rain go away,
Come again some April day;
Little Johnny wants to play.

Little Betty Blue, lost her holiday shoe;
What can little Betty do?
Give her another to match the other,
And then she may walk in two.

Here am I, little jumping Joan;
When nobody's with me,
I am always alone.

Solomon Grundy, born on a Monday,
Christened on Tuesday, married on Wednesday,
Took ill on Thursday, worse on Friday,
Died on Saturday, buried on Sunday,
This is the end of Solomon Grundy.

The man in the moon came tumbling down,
And asked his way to Norwich;
He went by the south, and burnt his mouth
With supping cold pease-porridge.

The North Wind doth blow,
And we shall have snow,
And what will poor Robin do then?
He will hop to a barn,
And to keep himself warm
Will hide his head under his wing,
Poor thing.

(COALS)

Black we are, but much admired;
Men seek for us till they are tired.
We tire the horse, but comfort man;
Tell me this riddle if you can ?

I had a little hen, the prettiest ever seen,
She washed me the dishes, and kept the house clean:
She went to the mill to fetch me some flour,
She brought it home in less than an hour;
She baked me my bread, she brew'd me my ale,
She sat by the fire and told many a fine tale.

Bat Bat *(clap hands)* come under my hat,
And I'll give you a slice of bacon;
And when I bake, I'll give you a cake
If I am not mistaken.

There was an old woman of Leeds;
Who spent all her time in good deeds;
She worked for the poor
Till her fingers were sore,
This pious old woman of Leeds!

Little Tommy Tittlemouse lived in a little house;
He caught fishes in other men's dishes.

As I was going to St. Ives,
I met a man with seven wives;
Every wife had seven sacks;
Every sack had seven cats;
Every cat had seven kits.
Kits, cats, sacks and wives,
How many were there going to St. Ives?

There was a little man
And he woo'd a little maid,
And he said "Little maid will you wed, wed, wed,
I have little more to say,
Than will you, yea or nay,
For the least said soonest men-ded, ded, ded.
The little maid replied,
(Some say a little sighed.)
But what shall we have for to eat, eat, eat,
Will the love that you are so rich in.
Make a fire in the kitchen,
Or the little God of Love turn the spit, spit, spit.

THE END.

In 1949, Dr. Edgar Osborne donated 2000 childhood books to the Toronto Public Library. This donation formed the core of the current Osborne Collection of Early Children's Books. From that original gift, fifty years ago, the Osborne Collection has grown to over 64,000 early children's books, games, manuscripts, archives and book-related original art, ranging from a fourteenth-century manuscript to modern notable English-language books. Open and free to anyone with an interest in the heritage of childhood, this world-renowned research collection attracts scholars and visitors from all over the world.
The publication of this edition of *Young Canada's Nursery Rhymes* marks the fiftieth anniversary of the founding of the Osborne Collection.

Young Canada's Nursery Rhymes had an interesting genesis.
In 1887, a book entitled *Young England's Nursery Rhymes*, with graceful illustrations by Constance Haslewood, was published in England, to the delight of English children. Three years later, in 1890, a shorter edition of the book, edited specifically for Canadian children, and entitled *Young Canada's Nursery Rhymes*, was published. During the editing process, twenty-one poems were deleted and for the line "In the month of February, when green leaves begin to spring," the first five words were changed to "In the merry month of May," to depict more accurately the Canadian climate. The favourite rhymes and jingles which had so delighted English children now found an equally receptive audience in turn-of-the-century Canada, and indeed they resonate in the universally beloved language of Mother Goose to this day.

The single copy of that original volume recorded in Canada is held in the Osborne Collection; it is worn and fragile. Using advanced electronic graphic capabilities, the publisher has faithfully reproduced the poetry and illustrations from the original volume, electronically repairing the most serious damage to the original materials, but striving to retain the visual appearance of the aged volume. This anniversary edition is very close to the edition that originally found its way into Canadian children's hands in 1890.

KEY PORTER BOOKS and the TORONTO PUBLIC LIBRARY are proud to present this Osborne Collection anniversary publication for the enjoyment of a new generation of young Canadians.